Let's Borrow a Book

"Can you read us a new story?" the Tweenies asked Judy one day.

Bella wanted a story about a princess, Milo wanted an adventure story, Fizz wanted a story about a puppy and Jake wanted one about a steam engine.

"I think we need to go to the library," Judy laughed.

At the library, Judy filled in the Tweenies' names and addresses on forms for the librarian, who gave each of the Tweenies a card.

"I'll stamp the date when you have to return the book in the front of it," he continued. "You can keep books for up to three weeks. Some libraries make you pay a fine if you keep a book too long, but we don't."

"So different libraries have different rules," said Judy.
"That's right," he replied.

"You can each borrow up to five books today," the librarian added.

"Why don't we borrow one book each today?" Judy suggested. "Five books each will be too heavy to carry."

Judy took the Tweenies into the children's library. There were books everywhere – on shelves and in book boxes.

NO RUNNING, RACING OR ROARING!

"Book-a-rooney!" yelled Milo, as the Tweenies rushed around the room.

"Shhhh," hushed Judy, pointing to a sign. "It says, 'No running, racing or roaring!' You have to be quiet in a library."

"The books are in alphabetical order, by the author's last name," Judy told the Tweenies. "It means we can find a book easily. If it isn't there, someone else may have borrowed it."

"What's an author?" asked Jake.

"The author is the person who writes the book," explained Judy. "An illustrator draws the pictures."

She led the Tweenies over to the picture books, where they sat quietly and looked at the books, until they'd each found one to borrow.

Bella chose a book about a princess.
Milo chose a book about an adventure.
Fizz chose a book about a puppy.
Jake chose a book about a steam engine.

But Judy's book was a secret.

They showed their books and cards to the librarian.

"Happy reading!" he said, when he'd finished checking out the books. "See you again soon."

The Tweenies couldn't decide which book Judy should read first.

"Why don't I read my book first?" said Judy. "I think you'll like it."

They wanted to know if it was about adventures, princesses, steam engines or puppies.

"Wait and see," she told them, pulling the book from her bag.

The Tweenies crowded round Judy to look at the picture on the front of the book.

"Oh, brilliant!" they cried, when they saw it.

"Shall I read it? "Judy asked them.

"Yes, please!"

So she did.

The Adventures of Princess, Puffer and Puppy

"We love the library," the Tweenies decided. "Can we go again soon?"

The End